187210

PowerKids Readers:

The Bilingual Library of the United States of America™

ARKANSAS

VANESSA BROWN

Traducción al español: María Cristina Brusca

The Rosen Publishing Group's
PowerKids Press™ & **Editorial Buenas Letras**™
New York

Published in 2005 by The Rosen Publishing Group, Inc.
29 East 21st Street, New York, NY 10010

First Edition

Photo Credits: Cover, p. 30 (State Nickname) © 1997 Digital Vision; p. 5 © Joe Sohm/ The Image Works; p. 7 © 2002 Geoatlas; p. 9 © William A. Bake/Corbis; pp. 11, 31 (Joplin, Jordan, Explorers) © Getty Images; p. 15 Library of Congress Prints and Photographs Division; pp. 17, 31 (Clinton) © Wally McNamee/Corbis; pp. 19, 31 (Festivals) © Hinata Haga/HAGA/The Image Works; p. 21 © Jen Taylor/VividPix; pp. 23, 31 (Library) © Roberto Schmidt/AFP/Getty Images; pp. 25, 30 (Capital) © Joseph Sohm; ChromoSohm Inc./Corbis; pp. 26, 30 (Apple Blossom) © Tony Bavistock; Eye Ubiquitous/Corbis; p. 30 (Mockingbird) © Joe McDonald/Corbis; p. 30 (Southern Pine) © Raymond Gehman/Corbis; p. 30 (Diamond) © Thom Lang/Corbis; p. 31 (Cash) © Neal Preston/Corbis; p. 31 (Elders) © Reuters/Corbis; p. 31 (Pippen) © Duomo/Corbis

Library of Congress Cataloging-in-Publication Data

Brown, Vanessa, 1963–
  Arkansas / Vanessa Brown ; traducción al español: María Cristina Brusca– 1st ed.
    p. cm. – (The bilingual library of the United States of America)
  Includes bibliographical references and index.
  ISBN 1-4042-3068-8 (library binding)
  1. Arkansas–Juvenile literature. I. Title. II. Series.

  F411.3.B76 2005
  976.7–dc22
                                                      2004029728

Manufactured in the United States of America

Due to the changing nature of Internet links, Editorial Buenas Letras has developed an online list of Web sites related to the subject of this book. This site is updated regularly. Please use this link to access the list:

http://www.buenasletraslinks.com/ls/arkansas

Contents

Contenido

Welcome to Arkansas

These are the flag and seal of Arkansas. Arkansas is known as the Natural State. It is also known as the Land of Opportunity.

Bienvenidos a Arkansas

Éstos son la bandera y el escudo de Arkansas. Arkansas es conocido como el Estado Natural. También es conocido como la Tierra de las Oportunidades.

The Arkansas Flag and State Seal

Bandera y escudo del estado de Arkansas

Arkansas Geography

Arkansas borders the states of Oklahoma, Missouri, Tennessee, Mississippi, Louisiana, and Texas. The Mississippi River runs along the eastern border.

Geografía de Arkansas

Arkansas linda con los estados de Oklahoma, Misuri, Tennessee, Misisipi, Luisiana y Texas. El río Misisipi corre a lo largo de la frontera este del estado.

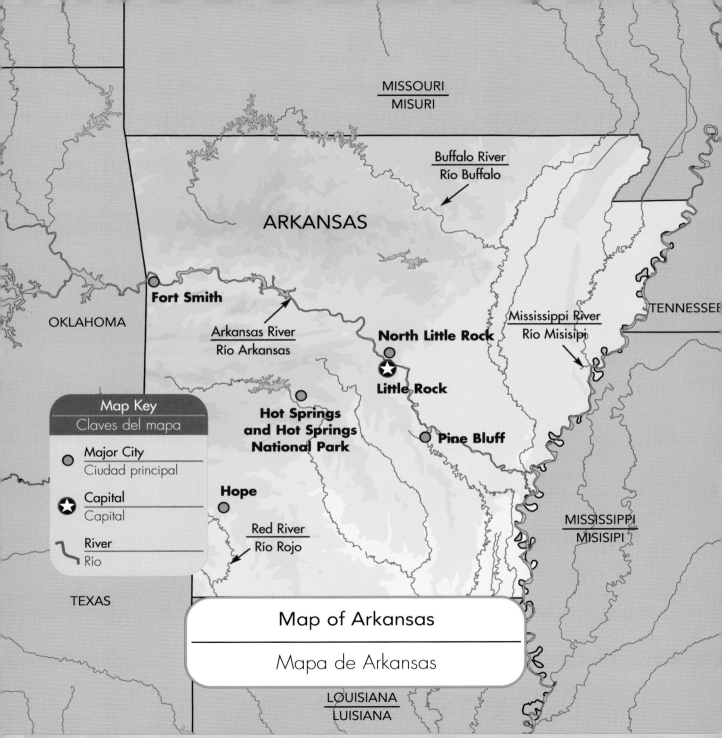

MISSOURI
MISURI

Buffalo River
Río Buffalo

ARKANSAS

Fort Smith

OKLAHOMA

Arkansas River
Río Arkansas

North Little Rock

Mississippi River
Río Misisipi

TENNESSEE

Little Rock

Hot Springs
and Hot Springs
National Park

Pine Bluff

Map Key
Claves del mapa

Major City
Ciudad principal

Capital
Capital

River
Río

Hope

Red River
Río Rojo

MISSISSIPPI
MISISIPI

TEXAS

Map of Arkansas

Mapa de Arkansas

LOUISIANA
LUISIANA

Arkansas is well known for its natural beauty. Arkansas has three national forests and one national park. In 1972, the Buffalo River was named the first national river in the country.

Arkansas es muy conocida por sus bellezas naturales. Arkansas tiene tres bosques nacionales y un parque nacional. En 1972, el río Búfalo fue nombrado el primer río nacional del país.

The Buffalo National River

El río nacional Búfalo

Arkansas History

French explorers traveled the Mississippi River in 1673. The French took control of the land around the river and named it Louisiana. This land included Arkansas.

Historia de Arkansas

En 1673, los franceses exploraron el río Misisipi. Francia tomó posesión de la tierra alrededor del río y la llamó Luisiana. Este territorio incluía Arkansas.

French Explorers Louis Joliet and Jacques Marquette

Exploradores franceses, Louis Joliet y Jacques Marquette

In 1803, the U. S. government bought Louisiana from France. This agreement was called the Louisiana Purchase and it doubled the size of the United States of America.

En 1803, el gobierno de los Estados Unidos le compró Luisiana a Francia. Este acuerdo se llamó la Compra de Luisiana. El acuerdo duplicó el territorio de los Estados Unidos de América.

The United States of America in 1803
Los Estados Unidos de América en 1803

Louisiana
Territory
—————
Territorio de
Luisiana

ARKANSAS

Daisy Bates was born in 1914 in southern Arkansas. She worked all her life to guard the civil rights of African Americans and women.

Daisy Bates nació en 1914, en el sur de Arkansas. Bates trabajó durante toda su vida para proteger los derechos civiles de las mujeres y de los afroamericanos.

Daisy Bates, Standing Second from Right

Daisy Bates (de pie, la segunda desde la derecha)

William Jefferson Clinton was born in Hope, Arkansas, in 1946. He was governor of Arkansas from 1979 to 1981 and from 1983 to 1992. He was president of the United States from 1992 to 2000.

William Jefferson Clinton nació en Hope, Arkansas, en 1946. Clinton fue gobernador de Arkansas de 1979 a 1981, y de 1983 a1992. Clinton fue presidente de los Estados Unidos de 1992 al 2000.

William Jefferson Clinton

Living in Arkansas

Arkansas is home to many fun festivals. The oldest festival in the state is the World Championship Duck-Calling Contest, where people try to make the sound of ducks.

La vida en Arkansas

En Arkansas tienen lugar muchos festivales divertidos. El festival más antiguo del estado es el Campeonato mundial de reclamo de patos, en el cual los competidores tratan de hacer el sonido de los patos.

Participants at the Duck–Calling Contest

Participantes de una competencia de reclamo de patos

Many Arkansans love music. The town of Helena is the blues center of Arkansas. The blues festival in Helena brings thousands of music fans every year.

Muchos arkansinos aman la música. El pueblo de Helena es el centro del blues en Arkansas. Todos los años, miles de aficionados a la música visitan el festival de blues en Helena.

The Blues Festival in Helena, Arkansas

Festival de blues en Helena, Arkansas

The Clinton Presidential Library in Little Rock opened in November 2004. The library honors to the life and work of president William J. Clinton. The library is also a museum and a park.

La Biblioteca Presidencial Clinton en Little Rock fue inaugurada en noviembre de 2004. La biblioteca está dedicada a la vida y obra del presidente William J. Clinton. La biblioteca tiene además un museo y un parque.

A View of the Clinton Presidential Library and Park

Vista de la Biblioteca y Parque Presidencial Clinton

Little Rock, Fort Smith, North Little Rock, Pine Bluff, Jonesboro, and Hot Springs are important cities in Arkansas. Little Rock is the capital of the state of Arkansas.

Little Rock, Fort Smith, North Little Rock, Pine Bluff y Jonesboro son ciudades importantes de Arkansas. La capital del estado de Arkansas es Little Rock.

The Capitol Building in Little Rock
_____
Capitolio en Little Rock

Activity:
Let's Draw Arkansas's State Flower

The Apple Blossom was named Arkansas's official state flower in 1901.

Actividad:
Dibujemos la flor del estado de Arkansas

La flor del manzano fue nombrada la flor oficial del estado en 1901.

1

Start by drawing a small circle in the center of your paper.

Comienza dibujando un pequeño círculo en el centro de tu hoja.

2

Then add five large circles around the small circle. Draw the shape of the flower's petals inside the large circles.

Añade cinco círculos grandes alrededor del círculo pequeño. Dibuja la forma de los pétalos adentro de los círculos grandes.

3

Erase extra any lines.
Connect the petals with the
center with small lines.

Borra las líneas sobrantes.
Conecta los pétalos con el
centro usando líneas cortas.

4

Draw wavy lines from the
circle. Draw tiny circles at the
end of the wavy lines.

Traza líneas ondeadas desde el
centro. Dibuja pequeñísimos
círculos al final de cada línea
ondeada.

5

Add shading to the flower
and you are finished.

Sombrea la flor y habrás
terminado.

Timeline

France claims ownership of the Mississippi River valley and names the area Louisiana.	**1682**
The United States purchases the Louisiana Territory.	**1803**
Arkansas becomes the twenty-fifth state.	**1836**
The Civil War begins. Arkansas leaves the Union.	**1861**
Arkansas is readmitted to the United States.	**1868**
Arkansas celebrates 150 years of statehood.	**1986**
The William J. Clinton Presidential Library and Park opens in Little Rock	**2004**

Cronología

1682	Francia reclama la propiedad del valle del río Misisipi y llama Luisiana a esta región.
1803	Los Estados Unidos compran el Territorio de Luisiana.
1836	Arkansas se convierte en el estado número veinticinco de la Unión.
1861	Comienza la Guerra Civil. Arkansas se separa de la Unión.
1868	Arkansas es readmitida en los Estados Unidos.
1986	Arkansas celebra sus 150 años como estado.
2004	Se inaugura la Biblioteca y Parque Presidencial William J. Clinton en Little Rock.

Arkansas Events

January to March
Thoroughbred racing
in Hot Springs

April
Arkansas Folk Festival
in Mountain View

May
Riverfest in Little Rock

June
Music Festival of Arkansas
in Fayetteville

July
Rodeo of the Ozarks in Springdale

September
Four State Fair and Rodeo
in Texarkana

October
Ozarks Art and Crafts Fair
in War Eagle
Rice Festival in Weiner

November
World's Championship Duck-Calling
Contest in Stuttgart

Eventos en Arkansas

Enero a marzo
Carrera de caballos de pura sangre, en
Hot Springs

Abril
Festival folclórico de Arkansas
en Mountain View

Mayo
Festival del río, en Little Rock

Junio
Festival de música de Arkansas, en
Fayetteville

Julio
Rodeo de los Ozarks, en Springdale

Septiembre
Feria de los cuatro estados y rodeo,
en Texarkana

Octubre
Feria de arte y artesanía Ozarks,
en War Eagle
Festival del arroz, en Weiner

Noviembre
Campeonato mundial de llamadores de
patos, en Stuttgart

Arkansas Facts/Datos sobre Arkansas

<u>Population</u> 2.6 million		<u>Población</u> 2.6 millones
<u>Capital</u> Little Rock		<u>Capital</u> Little Rock
<u>State Motto</u> The People Rule		<u>Lema del estado</u> El pueblo gobierna
<u>State Flower</u> Apple blossom		<u>Flor del estado</u> Flor del manzano
<u>State Bird</u> Mockingbird		<u>Ave del estado</u> Sinsonte
<u>State Nickname</u> The Natural State; Land of Opportunity		<u>Mote del estado</u> El Estado Natural Tierra de Oportunidades
<u>State Tree</u> Southern Pine		<u>Árbol del estado</u> Pino de hoja larga
<u>State Song</u> "Oh Arkansas"		<u>Canción del estado</u> "Oh, Arkansas"
<u>State Gemstone</u> Diamond		<u>Piedra preciosa</u> Diamante

Famous Arkansans/Arkansinos famosos

Scott Joplin
(1868–1917)

Musician
Músico

Louis Jordan
(1908–1975)

Jazz musician
Músico de jazz

Johnny Cash
(1932–2004)

Singer
Cantante

M. Joycelyn Elders
(1933–1994)

U.S. surgeon general
Cirujana general de E.U.A.

William J. Clinton
(1946–   )

U.S. president
Presidente de E.U.A.

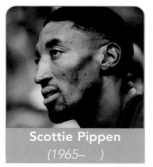

Scottie Pippen
(1965–   )

Basketball player
Jugador de baloncesto

Words to Know/Palabras que debes saber

border
frontera

explorers
exploradores

festivals
festivales

library
biblioteca

Here are more books to read about Arkansas:
Otros libros que puedes leer sobre Arkansas:

In English/En inglés:

Arkansas
America the Beautiful Series
By McNair, Sylvia
Children's Press, 2001

Arkansas
From Sea to Shinning Sea
By Fradin, Brindell Dennis and
Fradin, Judith Bloom
Children's Press, 1994

Words in English: 290

Palabras en español: 313

Index

Índice